S0-CBK-114

The Jungle Book

This book belongs to

_____

www.pegasusforkids.com

© **B. Jain Publishers (P) Ltd.** All rights reserved. No part of this book may be reproduced, stored in a retrieval system or transmitted, in any form or by any means, mechanical, photocopying, recording or otherwise, without any prior written permission of the publisher.

Published by Kuldeep Jain for B. Jain Publishers (P) Ltd., D-157, Sector 63, Noida - 201307, U.P

Printed in India

This graded series is written in easy-to-understand English. The aim is to develop reading habit in children and to increase their vocabulary.

One day, father and mother wolf saw a little baby crawl into their cave. They decided to keep him. They called him Mowgli.

Shere Khan, the tiger, wanted to eat Mowgli.

Father and mother
wolf would not let him.
Shere Khan did not
give up.

8

'The child of man cannot stay with the wolves,' said Shere Khan. 'Give him to me!' He told the leader of the wolves.

But Baloo the bear and Bagheera the panther decided to protect Mowgli. Shere Khan was not able to do anything.

Some years went by.
Mowgli grew up in
the forest. Baloo and
Bagheea taught him
many things.

'Be careful of Shere Khan,' said Baloo. 'He still wants to harm you.' 'I am not afraid,' said Mowgli.

One day, Bagheera told Mowgli that Shere Khan had turned the pack against Mowgli. 'Go to the village,' he said.

Mowgli went to the village.

He stayed there. He was safe. Each day, he took the bulls to graze.

One day, Mowgli's wolf brothers came. 'Shere Khan has vowed to kill you by tomorrow,' they said.

Mowgli was ready to fight Shere Khan. He knew the tiger would wait for him in the ravine. He made a plan.

Mowgli then took the bulls down the ravine. Shere Khan was surprised. He could not escape!

Shere Khan died as the bulls went over him. Mowgli then took off the skin of Shere Khan.

Mowgli took Shere Khan's skin to the wolf pack. The wolves knew that he had killed his enemy. They welcomed him back.

Mowgli was now happy.
After some time, he
went back to the village.
He did not return to the
jungle again.

New words to learn

crawl	tomorrow
cave	fight
decided	ravine
leader	plan
protect	surprised
careful	escape
harm	skin
afraid	enemy
pack	
village	
safe	
graze	
vowed	